CHAPTER ONE:
THE LIAR'S SON

They never said it outright. They didn't have to. Edrin Hale learned early that shame didn't need a voice. It lived in silences - longer pauses at the market stall, eyes that slid away instead of meeting his, conversations that stopped when his boots touched the square stones of Brackenford. The village had given him a name - *Liar's Son*. It followed him like a second shadow. He felt it most on winter mornings when the frost lay thick and the forest loomed dark beyond the last line of cottages. That was when his father had claimed to see it. That was when everything had gone wrong. Edrin pulled his wool coat tighter as he crossed the square, the breath from his mouth rising in pale clouds. Snow crunched beneath his boots. He kept his head down as he always did.

"Morning, boy," said Old Fenrick from the butcher's stall.

Edrin nodded. "Morning."

Fenrick weighed the meat twice before handing it over. The portion was smaller than it should have been, but Edrin didn't argue. Arguments required standing. Standing required a name that still carried weight. He tucked the wrapped meat into his satchel and turned toward home. That was when the laughter started.

"Oi, Hale!"

He knew the voice. It was the voice of Garrick Thorn who stood broad-shouldered, loud, and already wearing his father's confidence like armor. Edrin kept walking. He wasn't in the mood for a confrontation with him either. But Garrick wasn't finished.

"See anything white in the woods today?" he called. "Or is it only your kind that sees ghosts?"

Laughter cracked behind him like breaking ice. Edrin's hands curled into fists. For a moment, just a moment, he imagined turning around and saying, *"My father wasn't lying."* He imagined the words landing like arrows. But he had imagined that before. And they never landed... So, he walked on, still avoiding an altercation. He only wanted to get home to enjoy his meal. Their house stood at the edge of the village closest to Ashenwood. It had once been a mark of pride. Corvin Hale had always said a hunter should live where the forest could see him. That, more than anything else, set Corvin Hale apart.

Corvin didn't protest the name. He didn't defend himself nor did he warn Edrin away from it. He went about his days with the same measured calm he applied to everything - woodcutting, mending nets, or walking the forest edge at dawn. If the village watched him, Corvin didn't seem to notice. Instead, he told stories by the fire at night. Not excuses. Stories. Some were old, half-remembered things about the forest before Brackenford had a name.

Others were small and personal - where the river ran shallow in spring, which stones stayed warm longest after sunset. He never spoke of the day the village turned, and Edrin stopped waiting for him to mention it.

If Corvin felt the weight of the name, he bore it quietly. But Edrin carried it differently. For him, it was a living thing - something that shifted and pressed. It was something that changed shape depending on who was watching. He learned how to move through Brackenford without drawing attention. How to keep his head down and his voice even. He learned that honesty was not the same as truth, and that sometimes silence was mistaken for guilt. He also learned that the forest did not behave the same way people did. Now it was another reason people whispered.

Edrin stepped inside, stamping snow from his boots. The house was quiet except for the low crackle of the hearth. His mother sat near the fire with her hands folded in her lap. She had been beautiful once, people often said. Now, she looked like winter had settled into her bones.

"You're back early," she said.

"They were short on meat," Edrin replied, setting the satchel down.

She nodded as if that explained everything. Neither of them mentioned the village. They never did. Edrin's gaze drifted as it always did to the bow mounted above the hearth. It had been his father's. The wood was dark with age, and the grip was worn smooth by years of use. One limb bore a faint crack - a flaw Corvin had always meant to mend.

"I'll fix it someday," he used to say, but he never got around to it.

Edrin swallowed. "I'm going out," he said.

His mother looked up sharply. "Into the forest?"

"Just the edge," he assured her.

She studied his face, worry tightening her mouth. Then, she nodded.

"Be careful," she said, the same words she always used.

Edrin took his coat and stepped back into the cold to find Ashenwood waiting for him. The forest didn't avert its gaze when he entered. It didn't pause, whisper, or pull away. The trees stood as they always had. The paths remained where they were meant to be. Whatever judgment lived there, it didn't trouble itself with names. That was where Edrin felt most himself.

CHAPTER TWO:
THE STORY THAT WOULD NOT DIE

Ashenwood didn't welcome him. Edrin felt it the moment he crossed beneath the first line of trees. It was evident the way the light dimmed, and the air grew heavy as though the forest were holding its breath. His father had always said Ashenwood listened. That was part of the reason no one believed him. Edrin followed a narrow path that his father had cut long ago. Snow clung to branches overhead threatening to fall with the slightest misstep. The forest was quiet. No birds. No wind. Nothing. As he traveled deeper into the woods, he stopped at the old marker stone. Corvin had carved it himself years before Edrin was born. It was a simple symbol displaying branching antlers etched deep into the stone. Edrin brushed snow from the carving.

"They still think you lied," he murmured.

The words felt dangerous here. He remembered the night his father had come from the forest shaking; his eyes were alight with something between fear and wonder.

"I saw it," Corvin had said. "It was by the Frost Glade as white as moonlight watching me like it knew my name."

In that moment, a few people laughed not because it was funny but because the silence demanded release. Others shifted their weight, as if distance might undo what had already been spoken.

"I saw it," Corvin repeated, his voice steady. "At the northern bend just past the old ash."

Old Maelin crossed her arms. "Saw what?"

Corvin took his time before answering. He always did this when the shape of words mattered.

"The White Stag."

The name settled into the space between them. For a heartbeat, nothing happened. Then, the sound came. It wasn't a shout - at least not yet - but the shared intake of breath from people who understood exactly what they were being asked to do. His mother had gone pale. The village elders laughed.

"I know what I saw," Corvin said.

"You *think* you saw," Maelin replied, her voice calm in a way that made Edrin's skin prickle. "People think many things near Ashenwood."

"I didn't think," Corvin said. "It stood watching."   A murmur rippled outward. Details were dangerous.

"Did it move?" Garrick asked.

"No."

"Did it charge?"

"No."

"You didn't run?"

Corvin shook his head.

"You didn't pray?"

"No."

"You didn't call out?"

The questions continued. Again, Corvin's answer was no.

"What did you do, then?" someone demanded.

Corvin hesitated for a fraction of a second. Then, he calmly said, "I listened."

The laughter that followed was sharp and brittle. Someone spat into the road, and the space between people widened. Maelin stepped forward.

"Ashenwood does not give signs," she said. "It doesn't even choose witnesses."

"It chose my father once," Corvin replied.

"And he died for it," she said.

The words landed hard. Edrin felt his father's breath change beside him, and he felt the weight of an old accusation settle back into place.

"I'm not asking you to believe me," Corvin said at last. "I'm telling you what I saw."

Belief could be argued with, and truth demanded a response. Maelin's gaze hardened.

"Then you are either lying," she said, "or inviting judgment."

After that, nothing Corvin said carried the same weight.

Edrin knelt, pressing his palm to the cold stone. "I believe you," he said.

The forest answered with silence… then a sound. A single, distant note. Low. Clear. Like a horn calling across frozen ground. Edrin froze. His heart hammered as he strained to listen, but the sound did not come again. Snow slipped from a branch above him, landing softly at his feet.

"Just the wind," he whispered.

But Ashenwood did not feel like a place where the wind played tricks. Something else was present.

CHAPTER THREE:
THE MAP LEFT BEHIND

Bram Alder lived alone now in a cabin half-swallowed by the forest. People said that was punishment for believing Corvin Hale. Edrin approached the cabin and knocked once. The door opened before his hand could fall again.

"You heard it, too," Bram said.

Edrin stared. "Heard what?"

Bram's ears were sharp despite his years. "The call."

Edrin hesitated, then nodded. Bram stepped aside. "Come in, then. It's time."

Inside, the cabin smelled of smoke and old leather. He crossed to a chest and opened it before pulling out a folded scrap of parchment paper.

"Your father left this with me," he said. "He told me to give it to you when Ashenwood started calling again."

Bram didn't release the map at once. His fingers with pale knuckles lingered on the parchment.

"You don't go in thinking you'll drag the truth back by the antlers," he said. "The forest hates being handled."

"I'm not going to take anything," Edrin said.

He finally let go.

"Everyone says that," he said as he placed the map in Edrin's hands.

The parchment was warmer than Edrin expected, and the edges were soft as if they had been folded and unfolded a hundred times by uncertain hands. The lines didn't sit still. When he blinked, a stream bent where there had been none, and a stand of trees crowded closer to a path that had been clear moments ago. Marked deep within the forest was the same symbol of antlers. Edrin's breath caught.

"It's changed," he said.

Bram nodded. "It always does. Ashenwood won't be remembered too well. That's one of its mercies."

He turned toward the darkened window where the forest pressed closely listening.

"Your father understood that. He never tried to mark the stag's trail - only where *he* was standing when he saw it."

Edrin traced the antler symbol with his thumb. A low sound stirred in his chest. It wasn't quite a noise… not quite a thought… It was more like breath moving the wrong way.

"The call," he whispered.

Bram's mouth tightened.

"Aye, that just means the forest knows you're listening."

He met Edrin's eyes that were sharp as flint.

"Go in knowing why you walk. Don't promise what you can't pay. And if you see it - only once, mind you -don't ask it to prove itself."

Outside, the trees shifted just enough to make room for him. Ashenwood was not inviting him in. It was allowing him to enter - and waiting to see what he would leave behind.

"He wasn't lying," Bram said quietly. "But truth has a cost, boy. And Ashenwood always collects."

Edrin left Bram's cabin at dawn. The village lay quiet behind him, roofs dim with frost, smoke thin and undecided. No one stopped him. No one wished him luck. Proof was not something they wanted brought back. At the tree line, Ashenwood waited. There was no marker to say where the forest began. No fence. No stone. Just a place where the air cooled and the ground softened. It was a place where sound bent inward as if it were listening to itself. Edrin paused. *I'm here because my father told the truth*, he thought. At that moment, he felt the forest lean closer as if it were weighing the words. They rang clean enough.

When he stepped forward, the light shifted at once. It wasn't darker; it was *narrower*. The path he'd followed since boyhood thinned to a suggestion, then nothing at all. Leaves lay unbroken at his feet, though he knew hunters passed this way. Ashenwood didn't remember paths for long. The disappeared as quickly as they were created. He reached for the map. The parchment tugged gently in his hands - not pointing, not leading - only warming as if acknowledging he had crossed something that could not be uncrossed. A bird startled from the branches. Another answered. Then there was silence so complete it pressed against his ears. Edrin swallowed.

"I won't take you," he said aloud, unsure why the words felt necessary. "I won't drag you back like a trophy."

The forest didn't reply. But the air eased just a fraction, and the weight in his chest shifted - approval, perhaps, or simply permission. Then, he heard it. Not a sound exactly... More like the memory of one. It was a pull behind the ribs, low and patient, as if antlers were brushing the inside of his bones. *The call*. Edrin turned away from the village and the life that expected him to return emptyhanded - or not at all. His first step into Ashenwood left no print behind. And somewhere deeper within, something ancient took notice - not of his feet, but of his purpose - and allowed him to keep walking. Then, a sudden fear fell upon him as if he knew what lay ahead. In that instant, he spun around and sprinted home without looking back.

CHAPTER FOUR:
CROSSING THE THRESHOLD

On the morning the first snow came - late, thin, and uncertain - the world looked as though it had not yet decided what it wished to become. Edrin didn't tell his mother he was leaving. He stood in the doorway before dawn with one hand resting against the frame his father had carved years ago. The wood had smoothed with time and touch. The house slept behind him as the soft rasp of his mother's breath, the hearth's dying warmth, and the quiet that came only when grief had finished speaking for the night echoed throughout. The map Bram had given him was folded small and hidden inside his coat. His breath fogged the air as the cold bit through his boots and into his bones. The pain was sharp enough to wake him fully.
For a moment, he almost turned back. Yet, he pressed forward.

He imagined setting the latch gently, sitting at the table when the sun rose, and letting the days stack one upon another until the village's memory dulled. He almost chose safety over truth. Almost chose to remain Edrin-without-a-name... Then, Garrick's laughter rose unbidden in his mind - loud, careless, and cruel. He was reminded of the butcher's short measure and the way the scale never quite balanced when Edrin stood on the other side of the counter. He thought about the way his father's name *Hale* - once spoken with a nod of respect - had been worn thin and flattened into something brittle and false. It became a word that people tasted and spat away. *Liar's son.* Edrin stepped outside, and the door closed with a soft finality behind him.

Ashenwood loomed at the edge of the village, its trees dark against the paling sky. Snow had fallen in the night. It was light enough to soften the ground but not enough to cover it fully as if the forest meant to erase any sign of him without committing to the lie. The boundary stones crouched at the tree line half-buried, carved with symbols no one in the village bothered to remember anymore. Edrin stopped before them. No one crossed into Ashenwood unless they had to. Children were warned. Hunters skirted its edge. Stories of lost time, twisted paths, and voices that knew your name before you spoke it clung to it like moss.

"Fine," Edrin muttered, tightening his coat.

His voice sounded small, already swallowed by the trees.

"Erase me."

The moment he crossed the stones, the forest shifted. As his boot cleared the last boundary stone, something pale grabbed his eye. For a heartbeat, he thought it was snow wedged on bark, but the shape was wrong. It was too deliberate and too clean. Etched into the stone's far side half-hidden by lichen was the faint outline of antlers branching upward and worn nearly smooth over time. Someone had carved it long ago. Someone had tried to forget it. Edrin brushed his thumb across the mark. The cold bit sharply, and beneath it the stone felt warmer than it should have. He pulled his hand back. The village claimed the white stag was a story invented to excuse a man's wandering. Yet here, at the edge of Ashenwood, its shape had been carved into the very threshold as if crossing had always required remembering.

It wasn't something he could point to. There were no snap of branches and no rush of wind, but the air thickened, pressing against his chest as though it weighed his worth. The smell of pine and cold earth sharpened metallic and clean. The hush beneath the trees deepened. Though it wasn't silent; it was *listening*. Ashenwood was no longer just a place. It was aware. Edrin followed the map, although it behaved less like a guide and more like a suggestion offered by something that did not expect obedience. Paths twisted where none had been marked. Roots surfaced where the parchment promised open ground. Trees leaned closer together with their dark trunks narrowing his passage and their branches knitting overhead until the sky was reduced to a pale, distant strip. The map showed a stream where none should be; it was a bend in the path that refused to appear.

Edrin found himself drawn again and again toward markings the parchment did not explain. There were small notches and old cuts in bark that were always at eye level and always pale against the dark wood. Some were shaped like branching forks. Antlers. He tried to ignore them, but the forest didn't let him. He couldn't tell how long he'd walked seeing that time stretched strangely in Ashenwood. The sun never fully rose; it sat lingering low and wan as if it were uncertain whether it was welcome. Shadows slid in ways that made his eyes ache if he followed them too closely. Once - only once - Edrin heard the faint crack of something moving ahead of him. It wasn't a branch breaking or an animal fleeing. It was more like the sound of weight settling and stillness choosing a place to stand. He froze holding his breath, waiting for a second sound. None came. Yet the sense of being watched deepened. The feeling wasn't predatory or cruel, but it was measured. Appraising even. It was as though something ancient were deciding whether he was worth the trouble of being seen.

By what felt like midday, his legs burned, and his fingers had gone numb despite his gloves. His breath came shallow now with each pull of air scraping his throat raw. He stopped and knelt beside a narrow stream skinned with ice. The water beneath was dark and fast, moving with purpose. He broke the ice with a stone and drank. The cold seared his mouth and grounded him for a moment in something real. As Edrin drank, he noticed the stones below were a pale chalky white, smoothed into gentle curves that caught what little light there was and bent it upward. For a moment, the reflection staring back at him was not his own. Antlers rose where his head should have been. They were branching wide and luminous, their tines dissolving into the current. Edrin jerked back startled, and water spilled from his hands. The reflection snapped apart, broken by ripples. Only his own face remained - pale, hollow-eyed, and afraid of what it wanted to believe.

"My father didn't lie," he whispered, unsure now whether he was speaking to the forest or to himself.

The stream flowed on - indifferent or listening. And that was when the whisper came.

"Hale."

The sound slid along his spine, soft as breath against skin. Edrin spun, heart hammering, one hand already fumbling for the knife at his belt. Nothing stood behind him but trees and shadow. Then, he heard it again closer, clearer, and layered with a dozen voices that did not bother to agree with one another. *Son of the liar.* Pain flared behind his eyes, sharp enough to make him stagger. Memories surged - his father standing breathless at the hearth. His eyes were bright with wonder as he swore on everything that he had seen the white stag at the forest's edge. He thought about the village's silence afterward and the slow turning away.

"I'm not," Edrin said aloud, his voice hoarse and fragile in the vastness. "He wasn't."

The words felt small, but they were true. And he held them like a blade. Again, the forest didn't argue. This time, it laughed. Not with mirth, but with the sound of branches shifting and ice cracking with the deep, patient amusement of something that had seen truth fail before - and would again. Edrin stood upright. If Ashenwood wished to test him, then let it try. He set his feet, folded the map once more, and walked deeper into the trees carrying his father's name like a wound - and like a promise.

CHAPTER FIVE:
THE STAG-WATCHERS

They appeared at dusk from between the trees as though they had always been there and Edrin had simply failed to notice. The light had thinned to ash and silver, and the forest dimmed into layered shadow. One moment he was alone; the next, there were three figures where none had stood before. No snapped twigs announced them. No rustle of leaves. They emerged as the forest itself might exhale a thought. Gray and brown cloaks hung from their shoulders, heavy with age and weather, woven through with dried leaves, feathers, and small fragments of bone that clicked softly when they moved. Their hoods were deep, and their faces were lost in shadow, but Edrin felt their eyes on him - keen, measuring, and older than curiosity. Each carried a staff carved from pale wood and polished smooth by countless hands. Antlered symbols spiraled up their lengths, etched so deeply that they seemed grown rather than cut. Edrin's hand went to his knife.

"Easy," said the tallest of them, their voice low and steady, neither kind nor cruel. "If we meant you harm, boy, you would already be ash and memory."

The words settled heavily in the air, not as a threat, but a statement of fact. Edrin didn't lower his hand.

"Who are you?"

The figure tilted their head slightly, as though considering whether the question itself mattered.

"We are the ones who watch."

"The forest?" Edrin asked, his gaze flicking from one to the next.

"The truth," the watcher replied.

The word struck deeper than he expected.

"We are the Stag-Watchers."

At that, the other two began to move. They circled him slowly with their steps soundless on the forest floor. Edrin turned with them; his was pulse quickening and every instinct was screaming that prey did not survive inspection.

"You carry a broken name," said the first with its voice dry as winter bark.

"You carry a broken oath," said the second, softer and almost regretful.

"And you seek the White Stag," said the third.

Edrin drew himself straighter, forcing his shoulders back despite the weight pressing on his chest.

"Yes."

The word felt like a blade offered hilt-first. The tallest stepped forward. He was close enough now that Edrin could smell smoke and snow on his cloak.

"Then hear this," he said. "The White Stag is not hunted."

Their staves struck the ground once - *thud* - and the forest seemed to lean closer.

"It tests, and those who seek it for glory are devoured by their own desire. Those who seek it for proof are undone by doubt. And those who seek it to be *seen* are never seen again."

"I don't want glory," Edrin said too quickly. Then, he steadied himself. "I want the truth."

For a long moment, no one spoke. The tallest watcher studied him from the shadows with his head tilted, as if he was listening to something Edrin couldn't hear.

"Truth," he said at last, "is heavier than glory."

The other two raised their staves in unison. The air shifted. The trees to Edrin's left seemed to part - not moving, not bending, but simply *allowing* a narrow path to exist where there had been none before. Snow lay untouched along it, smooth and pale.

"If you pass," the watcher said, "you will not return the same."

Edrin's breath caught.

"Your father failed," the watcher went on as humbly as he could muster, "because he tried to carry the truth alone. He believed seeing it was enough."

Something twisted in Edrin's chest. Pride, grief, and understanding were all tangled together.

"Will I fail?" he asked.

The forest held its breath. The watcher didn't answer. Instead, the three figures stepped back, their forms already blurring at the edges and dissolving into bark and shadow. Leaves stirred where they had stood, and then they settled. In another blink, they were gone as if they had never been there at all. Only the path remained. Edrin stood for a long moment listening to his heartbeat to the quiet weight of what he had been offered. Then, he stepped onto the path and followed it, carrying his father's failure not as a warning - but as a lesson.

CHAPTER SIX:
THE TRIAL OF BLOOD

The path ended in a clearing choked with brambles and torn earth as though the ground itself had been clawed open. The trees ringed the space at an unnatural distance, and their trunks leaned inward but never crossed the threshold. Snow lay thin, trampled, and stained dark in places Edrin didn't want to examine too closely. Something moved within the shadows. Edrin smelled it before he saw it. Whatever it was reeked of rot, iron, and old rage. The horrid scent was thick enough to coat the back of his tongue. His grip tightened on his bow as the undergrowth exploded outward. Suddenly, the boar burst into the clearing with a scream that split the air.

It was enormous; its bulk was swollen and misshapen. It also had tusks that were cracked and blackened as though they burned from within. Its hide was a map of old wounds that never healed - gashes crusted over, reopened, and torn again. One eye was clouded and blind. The other glowed a dull, furious red. Edrin stumbled back as his heart hammered within his chest. *So, this is the test,* some part of him thought. As he stood with his feet planted in the Earth and his eyes focused, the boar charged.

He loosed an arrow on instinct. It struck true, burying itself deep inside the beast's shoulder… and didn't faze it one bit. The boar didn't slow, nor did it fade. It continued in Edrin's direction. Without second thought, Edrin tightened the grip on his bow and ran frantically in the opposite direction. Branches lashed at his face and tore at his coat as he fled the clearing with the sound of the boar's pursuit thunderous behind him. Snow sprayed beneath his boots. The ground betrayed him at every turn. He could feel the heat of the creature's breath now, and he could hear the wet rasp of it.

Unexpectedly, he tripped, and his world slammed into ice and pain. The bow skidded from his grasp. Before he could scramble back to his feet to continue his escape, the weight of the boar's shadow fell over him. It hovered with its tusks inches from Edrin's face. He screamed and brought up his knife with shaking hands. Then, he saw its eye.

Not rage.

Fear.

A raw, animal terror burned there - wild, frantic, desperate. It didn't display the hunger of a predator, but the panic of something trapped in a shape it did not choose. Then, a memory struck him sharp as frost. He envisioned his father sitting by the fire, voice low and steady despite the shaking of his hands. *Every cursed thing was once only human.* Edrin's breath hitched. This was not a beast to be slain. It was a wound made flesh.

"I won't," he whispered, the words tearing free before doubt could stop them. "I won't kill you."

The knife slipped from his fingers and sank harmlessly into the snow. The boar bawled, but this time, the sound fractured. It broke apart into something almost like a cry. The forest answered. Roots erupted from the earth, thick and living, coiling around the boar's legs and body - not in violence, but in restraint. Moss surged across its hide, bark blooming over torn flesh. The red glow in its eye dimmed, flickered, and then faded entirely. The boar sagged with its massive form growing still as the forest drew it downward, reclaiming what had been twisted.

When the ground finally closed, nothing remained but churned snow and silence. Edrin lay there, shaking, lungs burning, and tears freezing at the corners of his eyes.

The forest was utterly still. Then, far away a horn sounded once.

Clear.

Measured.

Approving.

Edrin closed his eyes as the sound settled deep into his bones. He had not won. He had been *allowed to continue*. The horn's echo faded slowly, thinning until it became indistinguishable from the wind moving through the high branches. Edrin lay still, afraid that if he moved, the forest might decide it had made a mistake. Snow drifted down settling over the torn ground, softening the violence of what had passed. The clearing no longer felt like a trap - but it was not safe either. It was *expectant*.

"You have passed the first trial."

The voice came from behind him. Edrin pushed himself upright and turned. One of the Stag-Watchers stood at the edge of the clearing, half in shadow, staff planted in the earth. The watcher's hood was drawn lower than before, but he felt the gaze clearly now. It was no longer measuring survival; instead, it was filled with judgment.

"That was the Trial of Blood," the watcher said. "And you failed it."

Edrin's stomach dropped.

"You did not spill it," the watcher continued calmly, "which is why you passed."

The watcher stepped closer, leaving no mark in the snow.

"You were offered fear and answered with mercy. The forest remembers such things."

Edrin swallowed.

"Was my father given the same trial?"

The watcher paused.

"Yes," the watcher said. "And he did not kill either."

Hope flared then twisted.

"But," the watcher added, "he believed that was enough."

They lifted their staff and struck the ground once. The clearing changed, and the snow thinned, drawing back as though it was ashamed of what lie beneath. The trees seemed to stretch taller as their shadows lengthened until they overlapped and darkened the space between them.

"Stand," the watcher said.

Edrin obliged.

"Now comes the Trial of Truth."

The air thickened. Not heavily but *bare*. It was as if the forest had stripped away every place a lie could hide.

"Speak," the watcher commanded. "Why do you seek the White Stag?"

Edrin opened his mouth.

"I seek to clear my father's name," he said.

The forest did nothing. The watcher tilted their head.

"That is not the truth. Try again."

Heat crept up Edrin's neck. "The village…"

"Does not matter."

His hands curled into fists. His pulse roared in his ears.

"I want them to believe me," he said. "I want them to believe *him*."

The watcher stepped closer.

"You want *vindication*. That is not truth. That is hunger."

The silence pressed in mercilessly. Edrin's breath shook.

"I'm afraid," he said finally. The words scraped like bone. "I'm afraid that he was wrong…"

This time the clearing *reacted*. Branches groaned, snow slid from boughs, and something deep beneath the earth shifted as though it were listening more closely.

"I'm afraid that he saw what he wanted to see. That I've carried his shame into this forest because I couldn't bear for his life to mean nothing," he stammered.

The watcher didn't interrupt.

"And I'm afraid," Edrin said, the confession tearing free now, "that even if the White Stag is real - *even if it appears* - it won't forgive him."
Silence filled the space momentarily.

Then, softly the watcher replied, "*That* is the truth."

The watcher lifted their staff.

"You have now passed the second trial."

Edrin sagged as he breathed hard in relief.

"But truth alone," the watcher said, "is a blade without a hilt."

They struck the ground again. Pain flared in Edrin's chest. It wasn't sharp. It was deep but and resonant. He gasped as a heat spread beneath his ribs as though something unseen had been pressed against his skin.

"What is this?" he asked.

"The Trial of Burden," the watcher said.

The forest darkened - not with menace, but weight.
"You may leave this place cleansed," the watcher continued. "The forest will carry what you have confessed. Your father's failure will not touch you."

Edrin's heart lurched.

"Or," the watcher said, "you may carry it forward."

Edrin looked down at his trembling hands.

"What does that mean?" he asked.

"It means you will not be spared. You will be a witness. Where corruption festers, you will feel it. Where truth is denied, it will burn in you. The forest will mark you as one who does not look away."

The heat in his chest pulsed.

"This burden will not make you loved or believed," the watcher continued.

Edrin thought of his mother, the village, the way belief had failed his father, and how silence had finished the work. He lifted his head.

"I won't ask to be spared," he said.

The heat settled into him like an ember banked deep beneath ash. The watcher inclined their head.

"Then, you have passed the third trial."

Far beyond the clearing, deeper than before, something vast shifted. Edrin felt it - not fear, not pain - but acknowledgment.

"The White Stag has not come to you," the watcher said. "That is not failure."
Not yet.
But *soon*.

They stepped back, already fading into shadow.

"It comes only when all three trials are carried beyond the forest."

The clearing stilled. The trees relaxed. Snow began to fall again - gently this time. Edrin stood alone, marked, emptied, and full all at once. Somewhere in the distance, a branch snapped.

Heavy.
Measured.
Watching.

CHAPTER SEVEN:
THE LIAR'S LEGACY

Edrin woke to frost clinging to his lashes and pain lodged in every muscle, deeply and unyieldingly. For a long moment, he didn't remember where he was. The sky above him was narrow, framed by shadowed stone. His breath came out in thin, white bursts. Then, the smell returned - earth, lichen, old bark - and with it the memory of the boar. The terror in its eye. The way the forest had risen in judgment. He pushed himself upright. The clearing was gone. In its place lie a narrow ravine; its walls were steep and damp, streaked with moss and darkened by age. A thin path wound downward between the stone faces, marked with small, deliberate stacks of pale stones. They hadn't been scattered by chance.

They had been placed.

Edrin's hand rose to his chest without thinking. Beneath his coat, a dull warmth pulsed faintly, answering the shape of the path.

"I know this place," he murmured.

The words tasted strange like they were part memory, part accusation. His father had brought him here once years ago when Edrin had been small enough to slip his hand into Corvin's without embarrassment. The gravel had shifted beneath his boots then, treacherously and eagerly to send him tumbling. *Don't run ahead,* Corvin had said, firm but not unkindly. *This path only holds if you respect it.* Edrin followed the ravine now, each step careful, weighted not just by fatigue but by something heavier - an awareness that this place remembered him, or perhaps remembered *why* he was here.

The ravine opened into a hollow. Trees rose in a perfect circle. Their trunks were pale and scarred, and their bark carved over generations with symbols that pulled at Edrin's eyes if he lingered too long. There were antlers branching outward, open eyes staring inward, and spirals that seemed to shift when he blinked. This was not a place made for walking through. It was a place made for standing still.

The air shimmered.

Edrin's breath caught…

And the forest took his breath away entirely.

He was no longer in the hollow. He was watching.

His father stood at the center of the circle. He was younger than Edrin remembered. He stood with his shoulders squared and his jaw set in the way it always had been when Corvin believed something fiercely and feared it would not be enough. Snow dusted his hair. His bow hung unstrung at his side. Around him stood the village elders with their faces hard, lined with something that wasn't wisdom. It was caution turned sour.

"You saw nothing," Elder Marrick said.

His voice was sharper here, unsoftened by time. "Ashenwood shows no mercy to liars."

"I saw it," Corvin replied.

His voice didn't waver.

"The White Stag. It watched me. It chose me."

The word *chose* echoed strangely as though the forest itself had leaned in to hear it again.

The elders laughed.

Not loudly.

Not cruelly.

Dismissively.

The sound cut Edrin deeper than Garrick's taunts ever had. This was the laughter that decided a man's fate and went home to supper afterward.

"You want to be remembered," Elder Marrick sneered. "So, you invent myths. You cloak your wandering in purpose."

Corvin's hands curled into fists.

"I wanted you to prepare," he said. "I wanted you to understand what watches us."

"You wanted to be believed," Elder Marrick replied. "And belief is not given to those who demand it."

The vision fractured.

Snow fell thicker now.

Corvin knelt alone at the edge of the hollow, his bow clutched uselessly in his hands. The trees loomed around him, immensely and unmoving. The weight of them pressed down unyieldingly.

"I only wanted them to understand," Corvin whispered. His voice cracked. "I only wanted to protect them."

The forest didn't answer.

Then—

The White Stag stepped from between the trees. Magnificent. Terrible.

Its coat was as pale as frost under moonlight. Its antlers were vast and branching, etched with lines that looked uncomfortably like runes - or scars. Its dark eyes held neither kindness nor wrath. Only judgment.

"You broke the rule," the forest said, not in words but in knowing.

Truth is not proven.

It is lived.

Corvin bowed his head. Not in defiance. In grief. The vision shattered like ice beneath sudden weight. Edrin collapsed to his knees in the hollow. His breath ragged, and his hands pressed to the cold earth as if it were the only thing keeping him whole.

"He wasn't lying," he said aloud, the words torn from somewhere deeper than anger.

Tears sizzled against the frost-stung skin of his face. "He was trying to do the right thing."

The forest listened.

It did not deny it.

But it did not absolve it either.

The warmth in Edrin's chest flared - painful now and insistent. He understood, finally, what the third trial had bound to him. His father had spoken truth *to be believed*. Edrin would have to live it - without asking for belief at all. Somewhere beyond the hollow, wood cracked beneath heavy, deliberate steps.

Not chasing.

Not retreating.

Waiting.

Edrin's knees ached from the snow, but he forced himself to rise. The hollow was silent now, except for the whisper of wind through pale trunks and the slow settling of snow on carved bark. He pressed onward along the narrow path that wound out of the circle. His muscles were stiff, and his chest tight with the weight the forest had left upon him. And then, a shape stepped from the shadow of the trees ahead cloaked in gray and brown with a staff in hand. It was familiar yet alien - another Watcher, though he had expected none. This one did not speak immediately. They simply observed. The way they stood, rigidly made Edrin feel the same scrutiny he had felt during the trials, yet sharper, heavier.

"I see you," the Watcher said at last, voice low and deliberate. "I see what you carry."

Edrin lifted his hands cautiously. "I…"

"You have been touched by the forest," the Watcher continued. "Yet, you still stumble under its weight. You speak of mercy, and yet your heart trembles with the need for others to believe."

The words hit him like a frost-laden branch. They were accusatory exactly - but they were filled with expectation and judgment.

"I…" Edrin faltered, struggling to explain. "I only carry truth. I've done what the forest asked."

The Watcher shook their head slowly. "Or perhaps you carry it too lightly. Or worse: you seek proof in its favor. How easy it is to fall into your father's mistake demanding belief where none is owed."

Edrin's chest tightened. He could feel the ember of the Burden pulse beneath his ribs, warmly and insistently. The forest had bound him to this truth, and now this Watcher misread him as greed or vanity, just as the village had misread Corvin.

"I'm not asking for belief," he said firmly, though his voice wavered. "I only carry it forward because it must be carried."

The Watcher's eyes narrowed under the shadowed hood. "We shall see."

With a step back, the figure melted into the trees, leaving Edrin alone with the hollow and the weight he bore. The path continued downward, steep and winding with each step echoing with the memory of the boar, the truth he had confessed aloud, and now this new misunderstanding. It wasn't just the forest that tested him anymore. It was everyone who would ever see him - the Watchers, the villagers, and the world beyond Ashenwood. And the forest had made it clear: the Burden was to be carried whether he was believed or not.

Edrin clenched his fists, letting the cold seep into his bones and letting the weight settle heavily but steadily. This was the inheritance of the Hale name. It wasn't glory. Nor vindication. Nor proof. It was responsibility. And he would not turn from it. The wind whispered through the trees, faintly, approvingly, or perhaps only acknowledging. Either way, Edrin understood: to walk forward was to continue the trial. And the forest would not release him again.

CHAPTER EIGHT:
THE SHARD OF WINTER

Edrin didn't know how long he knelt there. Time in Ashenwood bent like greenwood under pressure, stretching moments into hours and hours into a heartbeat. The snow fell lightly, yet no trace settled on him. It was as if the forest itself had paused, holding its breath. Eventually, he noticed the light. A pale glow seeped from beneath one of the trees, faintly but steadily as though the earth itself exhaled. Edrin approached slowly, every step weighted and every breath shallow. His pulse thrummed in his ears, loud enough to drown the whisper of wind through branches. At the base of the trunk lay a stone split clean in two. Between the halves rested a shard of ivory, long and curved, etched with lines that shimmered faintly like frost over glass. Edrin knew what it was before his fingers touched it.

The Horn of Winter.

Or what remained of it.

The moment he lifted the shard, cold surged through his arm sharply and clarifying as if ice itself had rooted into his blood. His mind felt unnervingly transparent; every fear, every hope, and every echo of guilt he had carried through the trials pressed forward. The forest could see through him. It knew.

A whisper stirred, curling around his ears, softly but insistently.

"Speak."

Edrin swallowed hard. His voice was small, but steady.

"My father told the truth," he said, the words carrying the weight of every trial he had endured. The shard flared brightly, casting white light across the hollow, striking shadows away from the carved symbols of the circle. Edrin gasped and nearly dropped it.

"My father was flawed," he continued, voice shaking, "but he was not a liar."

The shard pulsed in response with a heartbeat of frost and judgment. Then, it softened, leaving him awash in quiet light. He finally had proof - not the kind his father had tried to drag back to the village like a trophy, but living proof. Responsive. Judging. Hope surged through him, fierce and terrifying. He could see it now: the power to vindicate Corvin to show the village what they refused to believe.

"I can show them," he whispered. "I can clear his name."

The forest stirred not in approval but in warning. A shadow shifted in the periphery. The

Watcher who had misread him in the hollow of the ravine stepped silently into view, staff in hand, hood low. Their eyes glinted beneath it unreadable.

"You believe you understand what this gives you," the Watcher said softly, voice drifting like smoke over snow. "But the shard does not yield proof. It yields responsibility. And it sees all you carry - fear, hope, pride, and doubt alike."

Edrin tightened his grip. "I do not seek glory. I seek only the truth."

The Watcher's lips twitched, not quite a smile.

"Truth spoken aloud is dangerous. Even when it is right. Even when it is deserved. You carry the Burden, as your father did not. And still, you wish to show it to others?"

Edrin inhaled. Again, he remembered the boar, the confession, the warmth beneath his ribs that reminded him that the forest wouldn't spare him, and the hollow where Corvin's memory burned with the same fire he had carried.

"I carry it," he said finally almost in a whisper, "because it must be carried - not because I demand belief."

The Watcher inclined their head slightly - almost approving, almost warning.

"Then, you may walk forward. But know this: the shard will not shield you from misunderstanding nor will it keep your heart from breaking. The forest has marked you, and the world will test that mark."

Edrin closed his eyes; the shard cradled against his chest. The cold pulsed, steady and alive as if judging not just what he had done but what he *would* do. And somewhere, deep in the hollow of Ashenwood, the echo of a horn sounded faintly.

Not a call. Not a promise.

A question.

Would he carry it well?

CHAPTER NINE:
BELIEVED OR RIGHT

The dawn was thin and fragile like a held breath slowly leaking from the world. Snow whispered along the branches of Ashenwood clinging to dark trunks and brittle twigs. Edrin moved cautiously with his boots crunching softly in the frost and the shard of the Horn of Winter pulsing faintly in his hand. It was alive beneath his fingers as if it were aware of the weight of what he now carried.

And then it appeared.

The White Stag stepped from the trees without sound with frost forming beneath its hooves as though the earth itself were honoring its passage. Its coat shimmered like freshly fallen snow under the pale morning light. Its antlers branched impossibly wide, each tine etched with intricate runes that glimmered faintly, alive with ancient magic. The air itself seemed to hum, vibrating through Edrin's chest and bones. He dropped to one knee without thinking.

The shard burned cold in his hand. Every nerve, every sense stretched taut. His breath came out in trembling clouds. The stag's eyes, deep and dark as winter water, held him in judgment, weighing every intention and every heartbeat.

You carry what your father could not, the forest spoke through the creature. *Choice.*

Edrin's throat tightened.

"I… I want to bring the truth home."

Do you want to be believed, the stag asked, *or do you want to be right?*

Edrin frowned.

"Aren't they the same?"

The stag lowered its head slightly, and the shadows of its antlers stretched long across the snow.

If you bind the truth to proof, it said, voice like wind threading through pines, *Ashenwood will be forced into the world of men. Its magic will fade. The forest will become only wood and soil.*

Edrin's chest constricted. Every step of his journey pressed against him now - the boar, the Trial of Blood, the shattered visions of his father, the warmth of the Burden beneath his ribs. He remembered the Watcher's warning: *Truth spoken aloud is dangerous. Even when it is right.*

"And if I don't?" he whispered.

Your father's name will remain broken to many, the forest replied. *The forest will endure.*

He clenched the shard in his fist, feeling the ice bite into his palm. Memories surged like wind through his mind: Garrick's laughter, the butcher's short measure, the village elders sneering at Corvin.

And the Watcher who had misread him, almost condemning him for carrying the Burden rightly.

"What would you do?" he asked the stag, voice low and unsteady.

The creature's gaze softened, and a flicker of something eternal passed through its eyes. *I already have.* The forest held its breath, and Edrin felt the pulse of Ashenwood beneath his feet - a rhythm vast and ancient. The shard thrummed against his chest, steadily and insistently. Then… a sharp snap came from the tree line.

Edrin froze with his heart hammering. From between the trunks, a figure emerged, crouched low, bow drawn, arrow nocked. He moved like a shadow, silent and precise with his muscles coiled. Edrin's pulse screamed in his ears as the stag's ears twitched and its nostrils flared. The tension between man and beast was nearly visible, a taut wire pulled to breaking. Before Edrin could react, the hunter loosed the arrow. It sang through the frost-thick air striking the White Stag's shoulder. Frost sprayed from the wound, sparkling like broken glass. The creature let out a sound that was not a cry but the tearing of a soul itself.

"No!" Edrin screamed, spinning toward the hunter.

The stag bolted, hooves pounding snow, antlers sweeping low through the trees. Its eyes flicked back at him - dark as winter water, wide with betrayal - before vanishing into the forest. Edrin's hands shook as he gripped the shard.

"Why?!" he shouted, rage and disbelief crashing together.

The hunter stepped forward, chest heaving, bow still in hand, eyes bright with obsession.

"I've been following you," he said, voice tight. "I've tracked the stag for weeks. I thought… I thought you'd lead me to it. I would be the one to claim it… to prove it exists."

Edrin's chest heaved. "You… you'd strike it? For proof?"

The hunter's jaw tightened. "It's a legend. A trophy. The first man to claim it would be remembered forever. Don't you want to be remembered?"

Edrin's fingers tightened around the shard.

"You're blind. You don't understand. The White Stag isn't for glory. It isn't proof. You think you can own it, but you only destroy it."

The hunter's eyes narrowed. "And what? Let it walk free? Let it remain a myth?"

Edrin inhaled, letting the cold burn clarity into his lungs.

"It's alive. It chooses who it reveals itself to. It judges character not strength. You've broken something no one can repair with an arrow."

The hunter hesitated, seeing perhaps for the first time that Edrin carried something far heavier than a weapon: responsibility. Edrin raised the shard slightly, letting the light wash over the hunter.

"I carry the Burden. I protect what must be protected. Not for fame. Not for proof. Only because it is right."

For a moment, the hunter wavered as if he could sense the truth in Edrin's words and the forest's judgment behind them. Slowly and reluctantly, he lowered his bow. The snow around them was silent again. Only the shard pulsed, cold and alive, as if whispering approval. But the forest had marked the morning with betrayal. The stag would not return easily. It would watch, warily now, carrying the weight of human desire and misunderstanding. And Edrin would carry the burden of its absence and the knowledge that even right action can't always prevent harm.

He exhaled slowly. His shoulders were heavy but straight. The shard glimmered, steady in his palm. The forest watched. The hunter watched. And somewhere beyond the trees, distant and faint, the echo of a horn sounded as a warning, a promise, a question of what was yet to come. Edrin Hale would follow the sound. He would carry truth rather than a trophy. He would act rightly even if no one believed - even if the world tried to force him into proving what couldn't be bound. And somewhere deep in Ashenwood, the White Stag moved wounded but alive - its judgment yet to be rendered. Edrin tightened his grip on the shard and stepped forward into the forest ready to bear what was his and whatever it demanded.

CHAPTER TEN:
ASHENWOOD'S ECHO

Edrin stood at the edge of the clearing where the White Stag had fled. Snow crunched softly beneath his boots. His chest ached from the weight of what he had done and what had been done. The shard of the Horn of Winter pressed cold and unyielding against his chest, reminding him that some truths demanded action while others demanded patience. He had followed the stag for what felt like hours, stumbling over roots and frozen undergrowth. He was fatigued but driven by a mixture of hope and fear. Each breath came out in white clouds, and each footstep left a mark that seemed too loud in the hollow stillness. The stag had vanished, but its absence pressed upon him. He could almost feel its presence in the air - watching, judging, disappointed.

The forest itself seemed altered as the trees leaned inward as if they were listening. The faint crunch of ice under hoofbeats had long faded and was replaced by a silence that felt heavier than snow. Edrin sank to one knee staring at the pale impressions left where the stag had landed. The arrow's mark marred the pristine snow like a scar that refused to melt even under the weak morning light.

He whispered into the wind. "I didn't…"

His voice broke and became swallowed by the woods.

"I didn't lead him into harm. I—"

But even as he spoke, he felt the forest press against him. Not in anger but in expectation. Ashenwood weighed every word, every intention, every heartbeat. He could feel the ghost of the stag's betrayal like frost sliding over exposed skin. Edrin's mind replayed the moment the arrow struck. The stag's eyes - dark and brimming with disappointment - haunted him. It had not been afraid of him. It had been *betrayed by him*. He swallowed and gripped the shard tighter. The cold light pulsed, steadily and insistently, but it offered no answers. There was only the awareness of responsibility. He had been chosen, and with that choice came consequences beyond human understanding.

For the first time, he heard it. It was a presence brushing against his mind. And suddenly, the forest had become a whisper. *You sought truth. You acted rightly. Yet the world is fragile.* Edrin's heart thumped, the shard thrumming against his chest.

"I didn't do it for proof. I didn't…"

He paused as he inhaled and exhaled nervously.

"I only wanted to protect it."

The forest responded with a subtle shift. A branch fell softly somewhere far above, and snow scattered like shattered glass. The stag's aura lingered in the air, sharp and bitter as frost. He could feel the echo of its sorrow, and with it a new understanding developed: right action did not guarantee trust.

Edrin rose slowly, brushing snow from his coat. Every step forward felt heavier; each one a reminder that even victory carried pain. He slowly followed the faint, uneven traces of the stag deeper into Ashenwood. Hours passed, but the forest remained patient. Every twist of the path and every shadow seemed alive with subtle scrutiny. As he traveled deeper, Edrin's senses sharpened: the rustle of dry leaves underfoot, the soft sway of branches above, the occasional snap of ice as he crossed shallow streams all seemed so loud and clear. Yet the stag never appeared.

By midday, he came to a frozen stream where the stag's tracks ended abruptly. The arrow's mark had torn through snow and frost alike, and there, in the shallow water, the ice was cracked and scattered. Edrin knelt, brushing snow over the broken surface, feeling the forest's weight press on him.

"I don't know how to fix this," he murmured.

The shard pulsed faintly, and he felt the echo of the stag's spirit alive but wary, unwilling to trust so soon.

He remembered the words the creature had spoken through the shard: *Do you want to be believed, or do you want to be right?* The question now seemed heavier, almost cruel in its simplicity. He had chosen right, and yet… he had caused pain. Even justice, even truth, came with cost.

The sun dipped low behind Ashenwood's skeletal canopy as shadows stretched long across the snow. Edrin paused atop a ridge, scanning the forest.

Somewhere beyond the trees, he could sense it: the stag, moving silently with its presence distant, wounded, and watchful. He could not approach - not yet. He had to earn trust; he couldn't demand it. So, Edrin sank to the snow, hands clutching the shard, chest pressed against the cold. He let the forest and the stag's absence teach him. He understood now that the Burden was more than proving a truth to men. It was protecting life, guarding wisdom, and honoring the forest's judgment.

As twilight gathered, he heard another sound. This time, it was a faint crack of a bowstring behind him. He quickly spun around with shard held high and his heart leaping. The hunter from before emerged from between the trees; his stance was cautious but alert.

"I… I followed," the man said, voice tight with reluctance. "I wanted… I thought I could…"

His words faltered as he noticed the ice-cracked stream and the distant tracks of the stag.

Edrin's voice was low, controlled, but sharp. "You already tried. You almost destroyed what cannot be owned. There is nothing left here for you but blame and cold snow."

The hunter's eyes shifted nervously, glancing toward the faint outline of the stag deeper in the forest. Edrin could see both desire and awe in the man's face - the same reckless ambition that had struck the arrow before.

"This is not a hunt," Edrin said firmly. "You cannot claim it. You cannot own it. The forest decides who may approach and who may see, and you… you have already proven unworthy."

The hunter stepped back slowly, lowering his bow, though his fingers twitched with restrained frustration. He then shifted his shoulders as if something inside him had changed. Slowly, he reached back and unstrung his bow. The motion was practiced, almost tender. He didn't even look at Edrin while he did it. And when he turned toward the trees, the forest didn't part for him. It waited, and he hesitated at the edge of shadow. For a heartbeat, Edrin thought he might speak again, offer justification, bitterness, or anger sharp enough to armor himself in. Instead, he stepped forward, and the trees received him without ceremony. Branches closed behind his back. Snow slipped from limbs above, erasing the imprint of his boots almost as soon as they formed. The hunter didn't look back.

Within moments, the gray of his coat dissolved into the dim architecture of bark and winter light. The faint rhythm of his retreat - crunch, breath, crunch - grew softer. Then, it stopped. It didn't fade; it stopped. Edrin's pulse steadied. The shard pulsed faintly as if acknowledging his words. Night fell slowly, draping Ashenwood in frost and shadow. The stag didn't return, but its presence lingered in the whisper of the wind and the shimmer of snow along the ridges. Edrin knew he couldn't force it. He could only carry the truth and the Burden. He had to be patient, silent, and watchful. When he finally turned toward the boundary stones with the shard pressed close to his chest, he knew the forest had taught him something heavier than proof: *responsibility and restraint were the truest measure of courage.*

Brackenford awaited beyond the stones. Smoke curled from chimneys as life continued unaltered. The town wouldn't know of the stag's betrayal, the hunter's greed, or the lessons he had learned. But Edrin did. And he carried them, pulsing cold and bright, beneath his ribs like the shard itself. Deciding to pause his pursuit for the night, he began the long walk home. The forest's echo followed him, and the White Stag's shadow watched from afar, waiting for the day trust might be rebuilt.

CHAPTER ELEVEN:
THE WALK HOME

Edrin left Ashenwood at dawn. Snow drifted softly through the bare trees. The forest didn't resist him. Not a branch swayed to stop him. Not a whisper of wind questioned his passage. That frightened him more than any danger had. He had walked hours through the trees the night before, following the faint trace of the White Stag as it fled, wounded and wary. Each step through the snow had been careful and reverent. He had watched it vanish into the deeper shadows, antlers wide and glowing faintly in the moonlight, and he had known - he had *felt* - that its trust had been broken, at least for now.

The shard of the Horn of Winter rested against his chest, bound in cloth to protect it from the cold and the wildness of the forest. It pulsed faintly like a heartbeat under his fingers. Its light had dimmed when the stag fled as though it were mourning its pain and judging his intentions. Edrin's stomach twisted with guilt. He had done all he could. He hadn't struck the stag himself. He had acted with rightness and mercy, but even rightness could wound. And in the echo of its betrayal, he felt the weight of choice more keenly than ever.

The hunter… Edrin could not forget him. He had followed the man's shadow for part of the night, ensuring he would not make another mistake. However, the forest seemed to have claimed the hunter's ambition as it had the stag's trust. Even now, somewhere beyond the trees, Edrin sensed that same presence lingering quietly, being watchful, and still frustrated. It wouldn't leave so easily. Hours passed. The snow began to thin as the edge of Ashenwood approached. The twisted shadows of ancient trees began to give way to open fields. The forest's weight seemed to lift slightly, though a whisper lingered at the edges of his mind as a quiet, constant reminder that the world beyond these woods was small and ignorant. Yet, the choices made within it had consequences far larger than anyone could see.

Brackenford came into view by midmorning. Smoke curled from chimneys. The whiteness blended with the pale sky. Life went on unchanged and unaware that a boy had walked through a forest that tested the soul and emerged changed. Edrin's boots sank into soft snow along the outskirts of the village, and he felt suddenly small. The shard was heavy beneath his coat. And the forest, the stag, and the hunter all pressed invisibly against him. People noticed him before he could reach the square. Whispers rose like smoke from unseen hearths.

"That's Corvin's boy," one woman murmured, wringing her hands.

"Where's he been?" a man asked, voice sharp with curiosity.

"Look at him. It's like he's walked out of a grave," a child said, eyes wide.

Garrick Thorn stood near the well, arms crossed, smirk faltering as he took in Edrin's drawn face and the weight in his eyes. The boy's journey had left him older than his years, and he emerged more cautious and more aware of every glance. His steps didn't falter. He walked straight to the elder's hall, each heartbeat echoing the lesson he had learned in Ashenwood. Inside the hall, Elder Marrick looked up from his desk. His eyes narrowed as he regarded the boy who carried both the legacy and the burden of Corvin Hale.

"Edrin," he said, voice measured and cautious. "You've returned."

Edrin's lips tightened. He didn't speak immediately. The shard hummed faintly beneath his coat, a reminder that the forest's judgment was still alive and present even here. He drew a slow breath.

"I've returned," he said finally, "but I do not carry what you think I might."

Garrick's brow furrowed. "And what is that?"

"Proof?" Edrin asked, voice low and steady. "I have it. But it is not for men to claim. The forest, the stag… they judge differently than we do. What I carry is truth. Not spectacle. Not trophies."

The elder's eyes flicked toward the window where snow still clung to the branches of distant trees. Something unspoken passed between them. It was a recognition that the boy had walked through trials that would shape him for the rest of his life - trials no witness could truly understand.

Outside, snow drifted along the square, covering footprints and whispers alike. Garrick muttered under his breath and turned away, but

Edrin didn't notice. Instead, he felt the pulse of Ashenwood in his veins and the echo of the White Stag in his mind. He had failed to earn its trust fully, but he would carry that responsibility until it returned.

* * *

Later, as Edrin wandered the streets, he caught sight of movement in the shadows near the forest line. The hunter was still watching. Still hoping. Edrin's chest tightened. He didn't confront him at that moment - not yet. Patience, he reminded himself, was part of the Burden. He had seen the consequences of haste. He had seen what ambition without restraint could do. So, he simply let the hunter linger in the shadows. He let him watch. Let him learn what Edrin had learned in Ashenwood: the forest could not be commanded. It could only be honored.

By midafternoon, he reached the small clearing near his family home. Smoke rose from the chimney revealing a promise of warmth and hearth. He paused, letting the shard pulse faintly beneath his coat. The forest's echo followed him here like a quiet hum in his bones. He had survived trials of blood, judgment, and mercy. He had faced ambition - human and forest alike. And he had surfaced carrying a truth greater than proof. As Edrin stepped across the threshold of his home, snow crunched underfoot, and his eyes lifted toward the sky. Somewhere deep in Ashenwood, the White Stag still roamed, antlers brushing frost from the trees, waiting for the day trust could be rebuilt.

And Edrin Hale would wait, too. Not as a boy seeking belief. Not as a son seeking vindication. But as the bearer of a Burden older and heavier than any village gossip. He had chosen what was right, and that choice would follow him home - and beyond. The forest had judged him. The stag had judged him. And now, in the quiet of Brackenford, Edrin carried both judgments with him knowing the path ahead would demand more than courage. It would demand wisdom, restraint, and the quiet strength to do right when no one was watching. And though the villagers whispered, and Garrick sneered from a distance, Edrin did not falter. The forest had tested him. The White Stag had fled and judged him. The hunter had survived to bear witness to human ambition. And yet, he had emerged carrying the truth.

He was Hale.

And now, for the first time, he understood what that truly meant.

CHAPTER TWELVE:
TRUTH IN FROST

The morning was brittle, and the sky a pale smear of winter gray. Edrin stood at the edge of the village square, letting the shard rest lightly in his hands. Its glow was faint but steady like a heartbeat against the cold. He had wrapped it carefully, fully aware that even a whisper of its light could draw unwanted attention - or worse, misunderstanding. The villagers gathered slowly, curiosity threading their faces with caution and suspicion. Children pointed, mothers hushed them, and men like Garrick Thorn leaned from doorways, smirks fading into frowns. Edrin's breath came steady, measured. He stepped forward slowly, letting the shard hum faintly beneath his coat.

"I know what you've heard," he said, voice low but carrying across the square.

"That my father lied. That I am chasing ghosts."

He paused, letting the words settle like snow.

"I have been to Ashenwood. I have seen what cannot be claimed. I have walked where the forest tests the soul, and I bring back what it teaches - not for proof but for understanding."

Whispers rose. Garrick's lips pressed into a thin line, his arms crossed tighter. Edrin met his gaze and did not waver.

"You speak of myths," Garrick said finally, voice sharp. "We want proof. We want evidence not stories."

Edrin lifted the shard slightly, letting its pale light brush against the snow at his feet.

"Evidence is not the forest's way. Truth is not measured by what can be held in your hands. My father sought the White Stag alone and was judged. I sought it with honesty and restraint, and it still left me its judgment to carry."

A hush fell over the square. Even the wind seemed to pause, as if the forest itself were listening.

"You've returned," Elder Marrick said cautiously, "but what do you intend to do with this… truth?"

"I intend to honor it," Edrin said. "Not to prove my father right. Not to claim glory. To carry responsibility. To remember what must be remembered, even when it is painful."

A small murmur passed through the villagers. Some nodded uncertainly. Others frowned unconvinced. Garrick stepped forward, shadowed and tense.

"So what? You walk in with some glowing rock, and suddenly we are supposed to respect you? Respect your father?"

Edrin's eyes narrowed slightly, not with anger but with measured understanding.

"Respect is not given by evidence alone. It is earned through integrity, through action, and through choices that are seen - and unseen. I carry proof of my father's truth. But the forest does not allow it to be a weapon - only a guide. You may choose to believe or not. That is yours. But the truth exists whether you accept it or not."

Garrick's jaw tightened. "And the stag? Did it let you take it? Or did you drive it away?"

Edrin closed his eyes for a long moment, feeling the forest's pulse, remembering the stag's eyes, the arrow, and its flight.

"It is wounded. It left because it had reason to mistrust me as I had reason to mistrust ambition in others. I do not command it. I cannot force it. But I carry its judgment, and I carry its lesson: trust is not given lightly, and truth must be honored, even when it hurts."

Muffled chatter rippled through the square. Some villagers glanced at one another, reconsidering the stories they had repeated so easily. A few of the younger ones stared with awe, sensing a weight beyond their comprehension. Edrin took another step forward.

"I have returned to live rightly as my father tried to do and could not. My father was flawed, but he was honest. I am flawed, but I will be honest. That is all the proof anyone can truly offer."

The shard pulsed again faintly, and Edrin felt the forest brush against him through the veil of distance, the White Stag still watching and waiting, perhaps forgiving, perhaps warning. It was alive. It was real. And it had chosen to let him carry its burden for now. Garrick shifted, scowling but unable to deny the weight in Edrin's words. He glared, but there was hesitation now and a crack in his certainty. Elder Marrick studied the boy in silence, weighing him as he had never been weighed before.

Edrin exhaled slowly, letting the chill air carry his tension away. He didn't expect applause or praise. He expected understanding to come slowly, if at all. And that was enough. With that, he stepped from the square toward his home, the shard tucked safely beneath his coat, the snow crunching softly under his boots. Behind him, the village lingered in quiet speculation. Beyond the trees, Ashenwood waited, silently and patiently, watching the boy who had become more than himself.

Finally, Edrin crossed the threshold of his family home. His breath was still frosted, and his body was still weary. Inside, the warmth of the hearth pressed against him, yet the shard's pulse reminded him that warmth was not safety, and comfort was not certainty. He knelt briefly before the hearth, setting the shard down gently and letting its light mingle with the firelight. He didn't speak for words weren't needed. The forest had spoken. The White Stag had judged. And Edrin Hale had emerged carrying the burden of truth, tempered by restraint, aware of the cost of every choice.

Outside, the snow continued to fall softly and relentlessly. The world moved on. People whispered, speculated, and stared, but Edrin had learned what mattered. And for the first time, he understood: the path forward would be long, uncertain, and demanding - but he would walk it. Because he was Hale. And that was enough.

64

CHAPTER THIRTEEN:
THE BURDEN OF TRUTH

The morning sun barely pierced the low clouds, turning the snow into a muted silver. Edrin stepped out of his home with the shard of the Horn of Winter wrapped securely against his chest. He had slept little as the weight of Ashenwood and the White Stag lingered in his mind like a shadow he couldn't shake. The village square awaited, silent but alive with curiosity. People had gathered again, drawn not by whispers alone this time, but by the quiet rumor that something had returned with Edrin - something beyond mortal reckoning. Children pressed forward with their eyes wide while their parents hung back, guarded and watchful.

Garrick Thorn stood at the edge of the square, arms crossed, expression unreadable. Edrin's gaze swept across the faces. He did not falter. He had carried the forest's lessons, and he would not shrink from them now. Edrin stepped before them once more, not as a hunter returning with hope, but as a man who had looked upon the heart of winter and found it unyielding. His gaze moved slowly across the gathered faces, and there was no firebrand's cry in him now, only the quiet weight of truth. "You deserve more than tales of easy victories," he said, his voice carrying in the stillness. "The stag is no wandering beast to be driven by courage alone. It is bound to the cold itself, and the cold does not yield simply because we will it so. What we face will ask more of us than strength. It will demand patience… and a resolve that does not break when the snow deepens."

A hush fell over the crowd. Even Garrick's smirk faded, though his eyes remained cautious.

"I know what you want," Edrin continued. "You want proof. You want the forest, the stag, and to bow to your understanding. But the forest does not bow. The stag does not bow. What it gives is a lesson, and what it teaches is responsibility."

An elder woman emerged, hand trembling. "And what lesson do you bring?" she asked. "For us, for our children?"

Edrin took a breath, feeling the shard warm slightly beneath his cloth.

"The lesson is this: truth cannot be forced into the world of men. It must be lived. We must act rightly even when no one believes us. We must honor what is sacred, even when it cannot serve our pride. And we must carry responsibility for our choices, especially when we act with knowledge that others do not possess."

The shard pulsed again, sending a faint shimmer across the snow, and Edrin felt the White Stag's presence at the edge of consciousness - a distant awareness, watching, weighing, waiting. Garrick's voice cut through the silence, sharp and challenging.

"So, what do you do now? You've seen the forest. You've touched the magic. You return and lecture us? You expect respect for being a boy who wandered too far?"

Edrin met him, gaze steady.

"I do not expect belief. I expect understanding of what responsibility looks like. And I will not let ambition, greed, or pride undo what I have learned. I do not command the stag, Garrick. I cannot bend the forest. But I will act rightly in its name. And if you wish to follow me, you will learn that the forest does not reward haste or arrogance."

Garrick's jaw clenched, but he said nothing. There was a tension in the square, a quiet acknowledgment that Edrin spoke with authority far beyond his years, tempered by trials no one else could comprehend. Edrin turned to the villagers, voice softer now.

"I cannot force the stag to return nor the forest to bow. But I can bear its judgment. I can live with its lessons. And I will guide you to honor what is right, not what is easy. That is the legacy I carry from my father. That is the legacy I offer to you."

People in the crowd started talking amongst themselves again. Some looked at him with doubt still etched in their faces, but others nodded slowly as if they were sensing the weight of what he had said. A few of the children stepped closer curiously, seeing not a boy but a bearer of something ancient and vital.

*　*　*

Hours passed, and Edrin moved through the village listening and speaking quietly to those willing to hear. He didn't speak to win admiration. His aim was to plant seeds of understanding - small truths that might grow slowly over time into respect for what could not be held or conquered.

All the while, the hunter continued to linger with his bow in his hand. Edrin knew the hunter would act on his own ambition eventually. And when he did, the forest and the stag would judge him just as they had judged Edrin.

By afternoon, Edrin paused at the edge of the square, letting the shard hum faintly in the waning light. He closed his eyes, feeling Ashenwood in his bones, the pulse of the forest, the distant heartbeat of the stag. He couldn't call it back - not yet. But he could act rightly in its absence. He could carry truth where it would be lived not paraded. In the distance, Garrick moved away, his posture rigid but his expression less certain. The villagers returned to their routines - some curious and others beginning to understand. And through it all, Edrin walked steadily, carrying the shard close to his chest, aware of the forest's pulse, the stag's gaze, and the lessons he had survived to learn.

When he reached the boundary of his family home, he paused, letting the snow settle around him. Inside, warmth awaited. Outside, the world continued, unchanged and stubborn. But Edrin knew the truth now: the forest, the stag, the shard — they were part of him. And he was part of them. He had survived the trials, faced ambition, confronted doubt, and chosen the path of restraint, patience, and moral courage. The shard pulsed once more, a quiet glow against the fading day. Somewhere deep in

Ashenwood, the White Stag moved through the snow, wounded but alive, watching, waiting for trust to be rebuilt. And Edrin Hale - bearing the lessons of Ashenwood, the weight of his father's legacy, and the burden of truth - would wait as well. He stepped across the threshold of his home, the shard resting against the hearth, and exhaled. Edrin Hale walked on, deeper into Ashenwood, the shard steady in his grasp and the White Stag moving — slowly, deliberately — at his side. No oath was spoken. No triumph declared. The forest did not celebrate. It simply bore witness. That was enough.

Because truth, he had learned, was heavier than belief - and infinitely more necessary.

CHAPTER FOURTEEN:
THE RETURN TO ASHENWOOD

The snow had settled thickly across the fields. The village rooftops were completely white when Edrin made his preparations. He wrapped the shard of the Horn of Winter carefully. Each breath he drew was sharp, carrying the scent of frost and pine, a reminder that Ashenwood waited patiently beyond the boundary stones. He did not speak as he walked. There were no children to greet him and no villagers to stop him this time. He moved with purpose, each step measured, knowing the lessons he had learned - the weight of truth, the need for restraint, the cost of ambition. Ashenwood had tested him once. Now, he would return not as a boy seeking validation but as a bearer of responsibility.

The boundary stones loomed ahead, dark against the pale light. He hesitated for a heartbeat as he had once done, feeling the pull of the forest alive and aware. The shard hummed softly, almost imperceptibly, as if urging him forward. He crossed, and the world shifted immediately. Ashenwood was waiting. The snow beneath his boots hummed a deep, muffling sound. Trees stretched high, their branches heavy with frost, casting long shadows in the dim light. Edrin moved carefully, following the subtle markings Bram had given him. But more than that, he was following the pull of the shard, the quiet tug of the forest itself.

He didn't see the hunter at first. Not until a twig snapped behind him, sharply and deliberately. Edrin froze, his hand brushing against the shard. His senses were sharpened by Ashenwood's trials so much so that he picked up the faint rustle of cloth and the whisper of breath against snow.

"Back so soon, boy?"

The hunter stepped from behind a tree, bow in hand, eyes glinting with ambition and calculation.

"I've been patiently waiting for you to lead me to it."

Edrin gritted his teeth. "The White Stag is not for you to take," he said steadily. "I carry no map to it. You would find only ruin."

The hunter laughed lowly and dangerously. "Ruined? Or denied? You carry a piece of it in your hand, and yet you would lecture me? Step aside, and I will claim what should belong to me."

Edrin raised the shard, letting its faint glow reflect across the snow. "It does not belong to anyone," he said. "It chooses, it judges, and it teaches. You do not command it. I do not command it. We bear its lesson, that is all."

The hunter squinted. Then, he notched an arrow silently, raising his bow. Edrin's heart sank. He had anticipated confrontation, but not so soon and not so directly. He knew the stag was near. He had felt its presence in the pulse of the shard, a subtle shimmer across the snow, and a shift in the air. He didn't want to fight, but he could not let the hunter strike blindly. Thankfully, before the hunter could release, the forest stirred. Roots burst from the snow, wrapping around the undergrowth and anchoring trees with sudden strength. The hunter stammered, momentarily restrained by Ashenwood's will, but his intent was clear: he would not yield. Edrin moved, calmly and deliberately, positioning himself between the hunter and the forest's deeper heart.

"You cannot force its hand," he said. "If you strike, the forest will judge both of us. And you will carry its burden alone."

The hunter hesitated, and the tension in the air thickened. Then, with a sudden motion, he loosed the arrow. And it flew beyond Edrin into the clearing where the White Stag had been. The stag's cry shattered the forest. Edrin's stomach clenched. He had misjudged. The stag had been watching and waiting for a choice that had been made without it. The arrow struck, grazing its flank. Its eyes, deep and dark, filled with betrayal. Then, in a flash of frost and light, it disappeared into the deeper shadows of Ashenwood. Edrin dropped to his knees, the shard glowing faintly against the snow.

"Noo," he whispered. "I failed… I led it into danger."

The hunter advanced, bow still ready with a mixture of triumph and uncertainty in his eyes.

"It's your fault, boy. You brought it to me."

Edrin stood slowly, resolve hardening. "No. It is mine and yours to respect. You cannot take what chooses its own path. You do not understand its power. You do not understand its lessons."

The hunter laughed bitterly.

"Then teach me, boy. Or step aside and let me do what I will."

Edrin's eyes hardened.

"I will not teach you through compliance. I will teach you through witness."

He raised the shard again, letting it hum with cold light, pulsing like the heartbeat of the forest itself.

"You want the stag? You will have to understand it first. You will have to prove your restraint, your honesty, your courage - not your ambition."

The hunter froze, studying the shard, then Edrin. For the first time, he weakened, and uncertainty replaced arrogance. The forest seemed to lean closer, waiting. Even in its absence, the White Stag's judgment pulsed through the clearing.

"You will not see it until you have walked the path," Edrin continued. "And even then, the forest decides who may approach, and who is left outside."

For a long moment, the hunter said nothing. Then, slowly, he lowered his bow, steps hesitant, gaze guarded. Edrin did not relax or speak further. The forest would teach in its own time. The stag would decide in its own time. His responsibility was only to stand, to bear witness, to act rightly. The clearing was silent except for the snow settling on branches, the soft pulse of the shard, and the faint, almost imperceptible shimmer that marked where the stag had passed. Edrin knelt once, pressing his hand to the snow, letting the warmth of the shard seep through the cold.

"I will find a way," he whispered softly. "I will prove that I can be trusted. That I can carry the lessons you offer. And when I do, we will meet again."

The hunter fell back into the shadows, watching, learning - or perhaps judging. Edrin didn't turn to him. His path was clear. The forest waited, the White Stag waited, and Edrin Hale - bearer of the Horn of Winter, survivor of trials, warden of truth - would follow the path he had chosen. Snow fell softly around him, muffling sound and motion, folding the forest into silence. Edrin rose steady with deliberate steps. The pulse of the shard guided him deeper toward the heart of Ashenwood, toward the stag, and toward the lessons that had shaped him. And in that silence, the forest whispered, approving and warning at once. He had returned. And the journey - the real journey had only just begun.

CHAPTER FIFTEEN:
THE PATH OF REDEMPTION

The forest was quieter than Edrin expected. Each step left a crisp imprint in the snow, but the shadows of Ashenwood shifted in ways that made him doubt even his own feet. The shard of the Horn of Winter continued guiding him deeper into the trees. For a moment, he paused and closed his eyes. He could feel the White Stag's presence - faint, jagged, like a wound in the wind. It had fled, betrayed and frightened. Yet, it still lingered just beyond the edge of perception. Every instinct in Edrin told him to move carefully to honor the lessons of restraint, courage, and truth the forest had already taught him. The hunter was close. Edrin sensed it before he saw his shadow slipping between birch and pine, slyly. The man was skilled, patient, dangerous - but the forest had already begun to judge him, subtly and unforgivingly.

"Looking for it?"

The hunter's voice was calm - too calm - from somewhere behind a twisted oak.

"You think you can lead it back with that trinket in your hand?"

Edrin didn't turn.

"It is not a trinket," he said quietly. "It is a witness. And it judges every choice you make."

The hunter stepped into the clearing, eyes narrowed, bow at the ready.

"Then, judge me, boy. Or step aside, and I will take what you cannot hold."

Edrin's jaw tightened. He could feel the shard's pulse increasing, sensing the stag nearby. The forest shifted imperceptibly. Its roots curled just beneath the snow, and the hunter's steps grew heavier as if Ashenwood itself resisted him.

"You still do not understand," Edrin said, voice rising with quiet authority. "The stag chooses. Not you, not me. And it is not for your ambition or greed. You will not approach it unless you first prove your worth, not through force, but through restraint."

The hunter's lips curled in a bitter smile.

"Restraint? A boy lectures me on restraint while we chase a legend?"

"Not legend," Edrin corrected. "Truth. And you will destroy it if you do not learn humility."

For a long moment, they faced each other… two wills testing each other, mirrored by the silent trees. Then, the hunter lunged, bow raised, and released an arrow - fast, precise, aimed at where Edrin had last sensed the stag. Edrin reacted instantly, lifting the shard between them. A pulse of light erupted, scattering snow and wind. The arrow struck a tree, embedding itself with a splintering crack. The hunter stumbled, blinded briefly by the shard's glow.

"You will not strike again," Edrin said, moving forward. "You cannot force the forest, and you cannot command the stag. You will either learn, or you will leave."

The hunter straightened with a gaze that was furious but uncertain. He backed away, glancing toward the deeper forest. Somewhere ahead, the stag's presence trembled, its pulse weak but undeniable. Edrin followed, careful not to leave a trail that would allow the hunter to ambush it. Each step was deliberate; each breath measured. He remembered the lessons of the Trial of Blood: compassion over violence, understanding over reaction. The stag had not fled because of fear of him. It had fled because it had been wounded and betrayed by the arrow and the hunter's greed. He would need patience to rebuild that trust.

* * *

Hours passed. The forest deepened, branches knitting overhead, snow thickening. Edrin paused near a frozen stream, listening. The shard hummed faintly, a pulse echoing in his chest. He traced the trail of disrupted snow and subtle hoofprints leading to a ravine shadowed in pines.
There… The stag lay among the roots of an ancient oak, flank pressed against the frozen earth, eyes wide and cautious. It didn't move when he approached. It only sat watching and assessing as the frost formed around its hooves and breath. Edrin knelt in the snow, placing the shard gently before him, letting its glow wash over the clearing.

"I am here," he whispered. "I am not your enemy. I carry only truth, only care. I failed before, and I will not fail again."

The stag's gaze softened, though its breath came in sharp, shallow clouds. Edrin could feel its pain, the wound in both body and trust. He reached out, letting the shard pulse along its flank without touching the injury, letting the forest's magic mingle with the cold light.

"You were betrayed," he murmured. "Not by your choice, not by your will - but by someone else's greed. I will see that corrected. And I will not ask you to forgive me. Only to trust that I will walk rightly."

The forest stirred. Branches shifted, roots shifted beneath snow, as if observing, judging, and approving silently. And then, faintly, the stag lowered its head - nostrils flaring, ears flicking. Edrin could see the first spark of understanding, the tentative recognition that he had not led it into harm, and that he had acted with care. But they were not alone. The hunter appeared at the edge of the clearing with the wind at his back. He raised his bow, but Edrin did not flinch. Instead, he let the shard pulse brighter as the white light spilled across snow and bark.

"Step back," Edrin said, voice steady. "You cannot force what does not belong to you. Not by strength. Not by skill. Only by respect. You will learn this too late if you strike now."

The hunter hesitated, stepping closer but constrained by the shard's glow. The stag stirred slightly, flinching, and Edrin moved between them, eyes fixed on both predator and pursuer.

"You must choose," Edrin said. "Walk away, or face what the forest will teach you. I do not command the stag. I do not command Ashenwood. But the forest will act if you ignore its will."

For a long, frozen moment, the hunter's hand stuttered. He lowered the bow, a flicker of anger and comprehension in his eyes. Slowly, he stepped back, disappearing into the shadows, leaving Edrin and the stag alone. The pulse of the shard softened. The stag rose slowly, tentative, limbs trembling beneath it. Edrin remained still, letting the creature test his patience, his intentions, and his restraint. After long minutes, it stepped closer, eyes meeting his. There was no word between them, only understanding, the unspoken acknowledgment of trust begun, but not yet complete. Edrin knelt once, letting snow and frost settle around them.

"We will walk this path together," he whispered.

"Not as hunter and prey. Not as boy and legend. But as bearer and witness. And one day, perhaps, you will choose to trust me fully."

The forest sighed around them, a soft rush of wind through branches, and the faint shimmer of the White Stag's coat glimmered in the dim light. Ashenwood had tested him, the hunter had tried, and the stag had been wounded - but Edrin had endured. He had acted rightly, he had borne restraint, and he had walked the path of redemption. Snow fell softly and endlessly. The stag moved beside him now, hesitant but willing. Edrin felt the pulse of the shard steady in his hand. He would not force the bond, not yet. But the first step had been taken, and the forest was aware. Edrin Hale walked on, deeper into Ashenwood, heart steady, shard pulsing, and the

White Stag at last moving again beside him. The journey was far from over. The lessons had not ended. But trust had begun to return.
And in Ashenwood, beneath the watchful trees, that was all that mattered.

CHAPTER SIXTEEN: TRUTH RECLAIMED

The forest was quieter than usual, a heavy stillness settling over Ashenwood as though the trees themselves held their breath. Snow blanketed the undergrowth, muting footsteps and sound, turning the forest into a world of muted grays and whites. Edrin moved carefully, the shard of the Horn of Winter pressed to his chest. Its pulse was steady now, like the rhythm of a living heart, guiding him toward the stag. The White Stag had returned to the deeper forest, though its steps were cautious, each movement deliberate, eyes glimmering with frost and distrust. Edrin had learned patience. He did not call or chase. He did not speak except in whispers to the shard. He walked slowly, letting the forest judge his intent, and letting his own heart be the measure of his worthiness. But the hunter had followed. The man had not given up; he had not learned restraint. He had only hidden, waiting for a chance to strike. Edrin stopped. He did not turn. He let the forest speak.

"He is here," he murmured to the shard. "Do I confront him, or wait for the stag's judgment?"

The shard pulsed faintly, a reminder that choice belonged to the bearer. Edrin exhaled slowly. He had learned that the forest demanded action, but only when it was guided by truth and care. He stepped onto a small clearing, frost glinting on every branch. There, the hunter emerged fully, bow raised, eyes sharp with ambition.

"There it is," the hunter said, voice low, measured. "The prize of Ashenwood. Step aside, boy, or you will be left behind."

Edrin stood tall. "Step aside?" he asked quietly. "You would take what does not belong to you? You still do not understand what you pursue." The hunter laughed, bitter and tight.

"Understand? I understand enough. And if you do not move, I will strike."

Edrin's pulse quickened, but his hand stayed steady on the shard. He did not raise a weapon, did not reach for his knife. He let the forest guide him, the shard illuminating faint trails in the snow, whispering of the stag's location and the consequences of the hunter's greed.

"You do not command this forest," Edrin said, voice stronger now, carrying in the still air. "You cannot force the stag. You cannot command truth. You are not its master - only its witness. And yet you persist in your folly."

The hunter's fingers tightened on the bowstring. "Then show me the way," he said. "Or move aside."

Edrin stepped forward, letting the shard glow brighter. Light spilled across the snow, illuminating frost-laden branches and the delicate shimmer of winter in the forest. The stag emerged then from behind a cluster of birch, antlers tipped with ice, breath steaming, eyes dark and wide. It froze, watching them both.

The hunter's mouth fell open.

"It…" he began, but Edrin cut him off.

"Do not speak," Edrin said. "You do not yet deserve to witness it fully. You would force it with your hands, with your skill, and ruin everything. You have been tested, and you have failed. But it is not too late to walk rightly."

The hunter's bow twitched. The forest seemed to lean closer, roots curling just beneath the snow, as if ready to defend its ward. The stag shifted slightly, frost sparkling on its hooves, watching. Edrin knelt, keeping his hands empty, letting the shard pulse at chest height.

"I offer no command. Only witness. Only truth. Only care. Do you see it? Do you understand that your strength does not matter here? Only your choices?"

The hunter hesitated. He took a step closer, then another. He wanted the stag, yes, but Edrin could see doubt flicker in his eyes. For the first time, he felt the weight of restraint pressing on him, the forest's invisible hand guiding his conscience. The stag exhaled slowly, frost drifting from its muzzle. Its gaze shifted to Edrin, then to the hunter, and then back. It made no move forward and no step back. Only watched. Its judgment was silent, but absolute. Edrin held the shard out between them, letting its glow touch the snow at the hunter's feet.

"You may leave," he said softly. "And in leaving, you may learn something of restraint, care, and truth. Or you may stay and face the consequences of your own ambition. The choice is yours."

For a heartbeat, the hunter wavered. The forest seemed to hold its breath. Then, slowly, reluctantly, he lowered his bow.

"You are… stronger than I imagined," he muttered. "Not in skill, but in… understanding."

Edrin nodded once.

"Strength is measured in restraint rather than force. Now leave."

The hunter backed into the shadows, disappearing between the trees, leaving Edrin and the stag alone. The forest relaxed around them, a soft sigh through frost-laden branches, the pulse of the shard calming as though content with the resolution. The stag approached cautiously. Each step was measured, deliberate, and testing but not fleeing. It lowered its head near Edrin, nostrils flaring, breath mingling with his own. Edrin did not reach to touch it yet. He waited, letting trust build, letting patience do its work.

"You have learned," he whispered. "I have learned. The forest has judged, and we have walked rightly. Perhaps now… you may forgive me."

The stag's breath fogged the air, snow falling from its antlers like delicate tears. It shifted closer still, eyes locking with Edrin's. No words passed, but an understanding deepened as if time itself had slowed to watch the bond rekindle. Edrin knelt in the snow, letting the shard pulse at his side, a heartbeat shared between boy, stag, and forest.

"I will not force you," he said softly. "I will wait. I will bear witness. And when you are ready… we will walk together."

The stag nuzzled the air near him - a subtle acknowledgement and a bridge of trust forming. Edrin felt a surge of relief and reverence, his heart lighter but still steady with responsibility. Hours passed in quiet companionship. The forest watched, approving and patient. Snow drifted around them, coating trees, blanketing the ground, muting the world outside Ashenwood. Edrin knew that he had reclaimed more than just the stag's trust; he had reclaimed his own understanding of truth, responsibility, and care. Eventually, the stag moved, tentative but resolute, steps careful as it tested the forest floor. Edrin rose, letting the shard glow brightly in his hand, following it. The forest seemed to open paths before them, branches arching like protective hands, roots parting gently in recognition.

"You are not a hunter," he whispered. "You are a guardian, a witness, and a bearer of truth."

The stag paused, nostrils flaring. Then, it moved onward. Edrin followed, step for step; each movement deliberate, each breath shared, each heartbeat echoing the rhythm of the shard. They moved together through the forest, deeper than he had ever been, snow crunching softly beneath their feet. And though the forest had tested him, though the hunter had challenged him, Edrin Hale now understood what it meant to act rightly, to bear the weight of truth without seeking glory, and to walk the path the White Stag had set before him. The forest waited. The shard pulsed steadily at his side. The White Stag's gaze never left him. And Edrin knew, finally, that the trials were not over, but that he would walk them with integrity, courage, and patience –

always guided by truth, always guided by the forest, and always guided by the heart that bore the name Hale.

CHAPTER SEVENTEEN:
RETURN OF THE HUNTED
AND THE BEARER

The village of Brackenford had not changed. Smoke still curled from chimneys. The square still held its well and its gossiping villagers. And yet, for Edrin, the world seemed smaller and sharper at the edges, each stone and frost-laden roof carrying the weight of memory and expectation. He stepped onto the main street slowly, snow crunching beneath his boots. The shard of the Horn of Winter pulsed faintly still under his coat, reminding him of Ashenwood's judgment, of the lessons he had learned, and of the White Stag that moved through the forest beside him unseen.

Whispers rose immediately.

"That's Corvin's boy."

"Where has he been?"

"Is that… snow on his shoulders? Has he been walking in Ashenwood all this time?"

Garrick Thorn stood by the well, arms crossed, smirk faltering when he saw Edrin. Edrin met his gaze steadily, the calm pulse of the shard giving him confidence. He did not speak yet. He did not need to. The villagers had already seen the weight in his shoulders, and the seriousness in his eyes. This was no longer a boy chasing stories. This was a young man carrying the truth. Edrin made his way to the elder's hall once again. The heavy wooden doors loomed before him, carved with the symbols of the village's past. Inside, the elders waited, their faces tight with curiosity, suspicion, and perhaps faint fear.

"Edrin Hale," Elder Marrick said, voice sharp, but edged with disbelief. "You return. And you bring what? Tales of ghosts? Myths of a stag that does not exist?"

Edrin held the shard in his hand, letting its pale glow spill across the hall.

"I bring truth," he said. "Not proof as men demand it but living proof. The Horn of Winter remains. And the White Stag lives. It has chosen, but it does not serve ambition. It serves justice, witness, and patience."

The elders leaned forward, muttering among themselves. Skepticism warred with curiosity. Garrick snorted quietly, shaking his head. "So, it's true? Your father wasn't a liar after all?"

Edrin did not answer immediately. Instead, he unfolded the story of Ashenwood, of the trials, of the boar and the watchers, and of the hunter who had sought to seize what was not his. He spoke of restraint, patience, and the forest's judgment. His words carried weight, not because they demanded belief, but because they were measured, truthful, and alive. By the time he finished, silence had fallen. The shard pulsed faintly, reflecting in the eyes of every elder.

"Your father spoke the truth," Edrin concluded softly. "Not for glory. Not for attention. But because he saw what needed to be witnessed. And now, I carry his mantle, and bear witness as he once did."

Elder Marrick's face softened slightly, though he did not speak at first.

Then, with a slow nod, he said, "Then, the name Hale is… restored."

The murmurs began anew, but now with reverence rather than doubt. People stepped closer curiously, awe mingling with their skepticism. Garrick Thorn said nothing, but Edrin caught the brief flicker of respect in his eyes. Edrin left the elder's hall and stepped into the square. The snow glimmered beneath the rising sun. The shard pulsed faintly, a heartbeat shared with the forest beyond. The White Stag watched from the tree line, eyes deep, dark, and wise. For the first time, Edrin understood that truth and belief were not the same - but integrity and action could bridge them. Children approached, pointing, their voices soft.

"Is it true? The stag?"

Edrin smiled faintly.

"It is true," he said. "And it chooses whom it will reveal itself to."

The villagers watched him, and some nodded. Others still doubted - but it didn't matter. The weight of his father's name, the honor of the forest, and the bond he had forged with the White Stag were real, and they could not be undone. Edrin walked to the edge of the village where Ashenwood began. He paused and looked back once. Brackenford glimmered beneath winter sunlight, but his heart was already in the forest, among trees that had taught him courage, patience, and truth. Then, slowly, he stepped forward toward the line of trees. A soft sound reached him - the crunch of snow beneath hooves - and the White Stag emerged, majestic and patient. Edrin didn't call it. He didn't rush. He simply extended a hand, and the creature approached. It was not a pet, nor a trophy. It was a witness, a judge, a companion, and an equal. And in that moment, Edrin Hale understood that he had not reclaimed only his father's name, but his own place in the world - a place of honor, courage, and truth.

He turned back briefly toward the village. People watched from their windows and doorways. Some smiled. Some whispered. Some simply stared. Edrin nodded once, acknowledging them, but knowing that the heart of his journey was elsewhere - among snow and shadow, tree and root, magic and truth. The forest welcomed him. The shard pulsed, steady, and alive. The stag nuzzled his shoulder lightly, frost sparkling in the morning light. And together, they walked into the deep woods where the path was quiet, endless, and eternal.

The End.

EPILOGUE:
THE BEARER AND THE FOREST

Years later, the name Hale was spoken without doubt. Not because everyone had seen the White Stag, but because Edrin had lived with truth in such a way that it could not be denied. He often walked the boundaries of Ashenwood, the shard now faint in his hand, pulsing only when the forest needed witness. The villagers came to him with questions, concerns, even admiration - but Edrin always answered simply: truth is lived, not argued. Belief may vary, but integrity does not. Sometimes, at dawn, he would see the White Stag emerging from the forest, frost dusting its coat, eyes wise and patient. They did not speak in words, but in shared understanding. The forest was alive, ever-testing and ever-watching, but Edrin had learned to walk its path rightly.

Children would hear whispers of the boy who reclaimed his father's name, of the stag that roamed freely, and of Ashenwood, where the trees held secrets and the forest judged all who entered. And Edrin Hale, bearer of truth and witness of wonders, walked the line between forest and village, carrying the legacy of courage, patience, and integrity. The shard pulsed gently. The forest whispered in frost and wind. And the White Stag waited - not for glory, not for reward, but for the continuation of a bond forged in truth, earned in patience, and protected in honor. Edrin smiled faintly, lifting his eyes to the snow-lit trees. The path was endless. And he would walk it rightly, always.